English edition © 2008 Shanghai Press and Publishing Development Company

Chinese edition © 2007 Juvenile & Children's Publishing House

This book is edited and designed by the Editorial Committee of *Cultural China* series

Managing Directors: Wang Youbu, Xu Naiqing

Editorial Director: Wu Ying

Project Designer (Chinese): Qin Wenjun

Chinese text by Zheng Ma and Zheng Li

Illustrations by Miao Wei, Pan Xiaoqing, Wang Xiaoming, He Youzhi

Translation by Wu Ying

Editors (Chinese): Zhu Lirong, Sun Yiheng

Cover Design: Zhao Xiaoyin

Interior Design: Zhang Guannian

ISBN: 978-1-60220-963-3

Address any comments about *Chinese Fables and Folktales (II)* to:

Better Link Press

99 Park Ave

New York, NY 10016

USA

or

Shanghai Press and Publishing Development Company

F 7 Donghu Road, Shanghai, China (200031)

Email: comments_betterlinkpress@hotmail.com

Printed in China by Shanghai Donnelley Printing Co. Ltd.

1      2      3      4      5      6      7      8      9      10

# Chinese
# Fables & Folktales（Ⅱ）

Better Link Press

# Contents

一 yī 点 diǎn 不 bù 假 jiǎ

# Not One Bit Fake

Illustrations by Miao Wei

A fish farmer had a pond with many fish.

A kingfisher lived nearby, and came everyday to the pond to catch fish.

Of course, whenever the fish farmer saw the kingfisher, he would hurry to shoo it away. However, no sooner had the farmer left, the kingfisher would always fly back again.

3

The farmer hit upon an idea. He made a scarecrow out of straw, cloaking it with straw rain cape, and crowning it with a straw hat. He had this scarecrow stand guard next to the pond.

At first, the kingfisher thought the scarecrow was a real man, so he did not dare to fly over to catch the fish.

But after watching for three days, he saw that
the scarecrow never moved. Summoning up
his courage, the kingfisher flew over and sat
right in front of the scarecrow.

6

Seeing that even then the scarecrow did not move, the kingfisher boldly went on to catch and eat some fish. After his meal, he even went so far as to perch on the scarecrow's shoulder and sing merrily, "Fake man, fake man ..."

The farmer was very angry. Then he hit upon an idea. He disguised himself as the scarecrow, and stood beside the pond, motionless.

9

The kingfisher came again, and after a good meal, perched on the man's shoulder and began to sing.

In less than no time, the farmer caught the kingfisher in his hands. Now it was the farmer's turn to sing merrily: "I'm a real man. Look! I'm real, through and through. Not one bit fake!" The kingfisher was completely stunned.

# 造火拜师
Zào Fù bài shī

# Zao Fu, the Diligent

Illustrations by Pan Xiaoqing

Tai Dou was a famous charioteer. People far and wide acknowledged him as a master, but he did not easily apprentice young men to himself.

14

There was an intelligent and patient young man named Zao Fu. He ask Tai Dou to teach him driving, and Tai Dou agreed.

However, during the first three years of Zao Fu's apprenticeship, Tai Dou never so much as talked to him, much less taught him anything.

16

Nevertheless, Zao Fu continued to revere his master, doing all kinds of household chores. People even mistook him as a servant in the house.

Now that three years had passed, Tai Dou started training Zao Fu. He began by telling Zao Fu to practice walking fast.

Then Tai Dou set thin, small poles upright in the courtyard, forming a meandering path.

Although narrower than a human foot, Tai Dou could walk along the top of the poles quickly without knocking the poles down.

When Zao Fu tried it, he kept knocking down the poles.
Nevertheless, he kept on trying, and after three days he could
maneuver through the path as well as his master.

Impressed by Zao Fu's patience and perseverance, Tai Dou finally decided to teach him his driving skills.

Eventually, Zao Fu himself became famous as a master charioteer.

23

# The Unmanageable Bat

Illustrations by Wang Xiaoming

Once, when the Phoenix celebrated his birthday, all the winged creatures of the air went to offer their congratulations. All of them, that is, except the Bat.

Displeased, the Phoenix and his attendants went over and said to the Bat accusingly, "I'm the king of all birds. Why didn't you come and pay me homage on my birthday?"

Shaking his head, the Bat replied, "I'm a beast that walks on his feet. I'm not a bird, so I'm not under your rule."

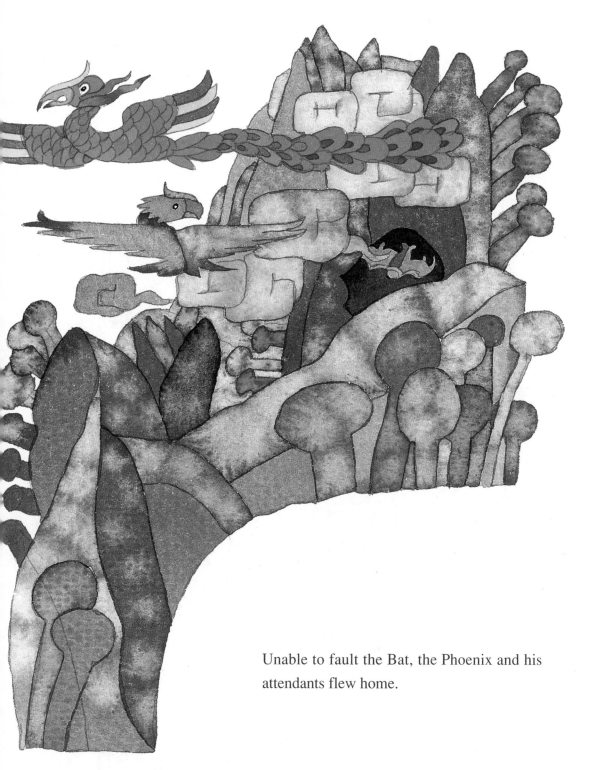

Unable to fault the Bat, the Phoenix and his attendants flew home.

Soon, the Kylin, the king of all beasts in the forest, had his birthday celebration.

All the beasts in the forest went to
congratulate their king. All of them,
that is, except the Bat.

The Kylin sent his minister Tiger to the Bat to inquire as to the reason for his absence.

The Bat replied with a smile, "I have wings and can fly. I'm a bird, so the Kylin is not my king. I don't have to go to see him."

The Tiger tried to jump up and bite the Bat, but he flew away, so the Tiger went back to report to the Kylin.

One day, the Phoenix met the Kylin in the woods.

The two kings talked about the sly Bat, but neither of them could think of a way to punish him.

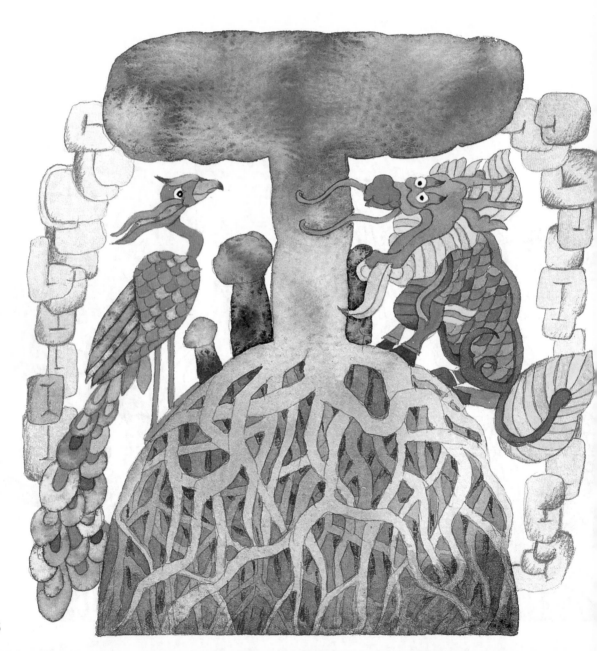

The Bat could not have cared less what they thought. He just would not be controlled by others.

# 截 jié 竹 zhú 入 rù 城 chéng

# Cut the Long Pole in Half to Get inside the City

Illustrations by He Youzhi

A man from the State of Lu once tried to enter the city while carrying a long pole in his hands.

But the pole was longer than the height of the
city gate, so he could not go through the gate
if he held the pole upright.

41

The pole was also longer than the width of the city gate, so he could not go through the gate if he held the pole in front of him, parallel to the ground.

The man was greatly perplexed by the fact that he could not enter the city while holding the pole either vertically or horizontally in front of him. He stood there scratching his head.

A kind-hearted old man suggested,
"Get a saw and cut the pole in two,
and your problem is solved!"

Wonderful idea! The man hurried to borrow a saw.

Zzzz, zzzz, zzzz, he sawed the pole in half.

Ha! Ha! Ha! The man from Lu went
inside the city.